D1613798

Girls Dance, Boys Fiddle

by Carole Lindstrom • Illustrated by Kimberly McKay

Pemmican Publications gratefully acknowledges the assistance accorded to its publishing program
by the Manitoba Arts Council, the Province of Manitoba – Department of Culture, Heritage
and Tourism, Canada Council for the Arts and Canadian Heritage – Canada Book Fund.

Printed and Bound in Canada.
First printing: 2013

Library and Archives Canada Cataloguing in Publication

Lindstrom, Carole, 1964-, author
    Girls dance, boy fiddle / written by Carole Lindstrom ; illustrated by Kimberly McKay.

ISBN 978-1-894717-82-3 (pbk.)

    I. McKay, Kimberly, 1968-, illustrator II. Title.

PZ7.L6623Gi 2013   j813'.6   C2013-904747-6

**PEMMICAN
PUBLICATIONS
INC.**

Committed to the promotion of Metis culture and heritage

150 Henry Avenue
Winnipeg, Manitoba, Canada
R3B 0J7

www.pemmicanpublications.ca

 Canadian   Patrimoine
Heritage   canadien

 Canada Council   Conseil des Arts
for the Arts   du Canada

 MANITOBA ARTS COUNCIL
CONSEIL DES ARTS DU MANITOBA

 Manitoba

To Sam – always let your heart soar and be filled with the proud heritage
of our Metis people.

"PEPERE'S TEACHING ME to play the fiddle for Memere's bush dance," said Metisse, as she reached for more fry bread.

Metisse saw Mawmaw and Pawpaw give each other the look. "We were thinking you would be dancing, not playing the fiddle," Pawpaw said.

"Yes, dear, we want you to learn the Butterfly Dance to surprise Memere," Mawmaw said. "It would be a nice way to honour her for her birthday."

"BUT I WANT TO fiddle," said Metisse, feeling her throat tighten.

"Girls dance, boys fiddle," Mawmaw told her. "It would be good for you to learn some of your heritage."

"Yes, Mawmaw," whispered Metisse, excusing herself from the table.

METISSE SAT UNDER her favorite oak tree. Slipping off her shoes, she ran her toes through the soft grass. *I can't let Memere down by not dancing for her,* she thought. *But I want to play the fiddle. If they could hear me play and see how the spirit moves inside me when I hold the bow and fiddle, I'm sure they would understand why I must play.*

She made her decision: she would do both.

EVERY DAY AFTER SCHOOL Metisse practised the Butterfly Dance with Mawmaw. "We're going to work on jigging today," Mawmaw said. "Let's start with the second part and see how you do." Mawmaw started the video and slowly moved through the steps to show Metisse.

"Your turn. We'll start slow and work up to faster."

METISSE PLODDED THROUGH the slow steps, missing the beat and losing her place in the music.

"It's no use, I just don't have any rhythm when it comes to dancing," Metisse fretted. Her moccasins seemed to have no problem moving in time when she was playing the fiddle.

"You're like the loon, clumsy on land," Mawmaw said, laughing. "You just need more practice."

But it seemed no matter how many times Metisse tried, she still couldn't glide across the floor like other dancers.

ON HER WAY to Pepere's house she ran into Mon nook.

"How's the dancing coming?" he asked.

"Not so good. I have two left feet," she said. "I'll tell you a little secret: Pepere's teaching me to fiddle so I can play at the dance," she said with excitement.

"Girls dance, boys fiddle," said Mon nook, laughing, as he ruffled her long, black hair.

EVERY NIGHT AFTER DANCE practice, Metisse continued her lessons with Pepere. Each new day the bow seemed to scratch and shriek a little less, and to Metisse's amazement it was soon gliding across the strings with little effort. Her feet kept time to the rhythm of the fiddle and she wasn't tripping or losing her place in the music, the way she did when she was dancing. After her third day of listening to Pepere play the Duck Dance she could play it completely through, even adding her own extra beats to liven up the music and make it her own.

Pepere could feel the spirit of the ancestors flow through him when Metisse drew the bow across the strings, and he knew in that moment that her voice was through the fiddle, not the dance.

"You're just like the loon," said Pepere. "Both of you make music that can rouse the soul."

It wasn't long before Metisse was playing two, even three strings at one time. Some fiddlers need years to learn to play more than one string at a time, Pepere told her.

THE NEXT DAY at school, Metisse listened to her friends giggle excitedly about the upcoming dance and the colourful clothes they would wear.

"I'm going to play the fiddle," said Metisse, puffing up her chest.

"Girls dance, boys fiddle," they said.

Why does everyone say that? she thought, hanging her head.

THE NIGHT BEFORE the dance, Mawmaw called Metisse to her room. "I have something I want to give you," she said. Mawmaw opened the old, worn chest and took out a delicately folded cloth. She unfolded the vibrant material with care. "This was my shawl when I danced my first Butterfly Dance," she said. "It was Memere's when she was a little girl. I want you to wear it tomorrow."

"It's so pretty," whispered Metisse, as Mawmaw laid it in her outstretched arms. She knew she'd be even more nervous wearing Memere's shawl.

AT THE DANCE, it was time for Metisse and the others to perform the Butterfly Dance.
I know why they call it the Butterfly Dance, she thought. Because I have so many butterflies
in my stomach.

The fiddle music started, with hands clapping and feet tapping. Metisse and the other dancers began promenading around the floor, do-si-do-ing as the fiddler changed tunes. As the music grew faster, the dancers unfolded their brightly coloured wings to the beat of the music. Metisse tried to flutter her shawl around like a butterfly wing, but it tangled around her legs, and she tripped into another dancer. Her cheeks grew hot as she struggled to keep up with the tempo, her moccasins dragging on the wood floor. Friends around her looked alarmed. They whispered to her what to do next, but she couldn't hear them over the music. It seemed that only when she was playing the fiddle could she keep time to the beat.

WHEN THE DANCE ended, Metisse could feel the tears welling in her eyes. Memere and Pepere gave her a hug. "That was lovely, dear," said Memere.

But Metisse knew she'd let them down.

"I tried my best, but I have two left feet." Wanting to be alone, she headed for the door, grabbing her fiddle case on the way.

WITH NO ONE AROUND to see, Metisse tried to mimic the dance steps she'd practised for the past few weeks. Her left foot got tangled with her right, and soon she was lying in the grass. There, she spotted her fiddle case. Wiping her moist eyes with her hand, she picked up her fiddle. She plucked the bow against the strings, and this time her feet had no problem keeping rhythm to the music.

METISSE COULD HEAR in the hall that it was time for the next dance. Her turn. She made her way up to the microphone, holding her fiddle case. Whispers and snickers could be heard from the audience. Carefully she removed the fiddle from its nest. The crowd grew quiet in anticipation. The bow soared across the strings as Metisse's fingers became one with the fiddle. She played a spirited Red River Jig as her fingers plucked the strings and feet tapped to the rhythm, Memere's shawl wrapped tightly around her waist.

PAWPAW SPRUNG UP and reached for Mawmaw's hand. He spun her around the dance floor.

The spirit of their ancestors resonated from the strings. Mawmaw and Pawpaw caught the spirit of the music. Memere was tap, tap, tapping her feet to the music. Even brother was clapping, keeping time with the beat.

Lights and shadows spun faster and faster with the tempo of the dancers' feet. Loud laughter mixed with the fiddle's shriek as the music of trembling strings filled the air.

THE SONG ENDED with a flourish and the crowd erupted with applause. Everyone crowded around Metisse, hugging and kissing her. Even her brother patted her on the back.

Metisse beamed. "I told you, some girls dance, and some girls play the fiddle."

GLOSSARY

Pepere – grandfather   **Mawmaw** – mother
Pawpaw – father   **Memere** – grandma
Mon nook – uncle

Bush dances – or house parties, which would occur when people felt like visiting. Women brought food and drink and the men played music. Sometimes the parties would arrive at someone's house, unannounced. The furniture would be pushed up against the walls to make room for a dance floor.

Butterfly Dance – a popular dance at Bush Dances. Three people would promenade around the floor during a tune and they would do-si-do in place when the fiddler changed tunes. The dancers wore brightly coloured shawls that they moved like wings. The fiddler controlled the length and pattern of the promenade.

Fiddle – the most common instrument used by Metis, and the core of their identity. Metis fiddle music is a blend of Scottish, French and Aboriginal influences that began in the early fur trade days in Canada. Though highly irregular in form, it is also highly rhythmic, with the fiddler often accompanying the music with clogging.

Metis enjoyed socializing, and placed great emphasis on relationships and friendships. Social activities at home drew people together for mutual support, comfort and celebration. Music was always an important part of these gatherings, and the fiddle would always be included. These activities promoted a sense of communal identity for a people who were semi-nomadic and who welcomed opportunities to gather with friends and family.

Red River Jig – the unofficial Metis anthem. Originating in the Red River settlement around 1860, it was thought to be composed as the tune for the wedding dance of a Metis couple. It is played at all Metis functions, and is the most popular and recognized Metis dance. It involves the shuffling of moccasined feet forward, backward and to the sides, to the accompaniment of the fiddle. The objective is to maintain lively, shuffling footwork while keeping the upper body as motionless as possible. Although the Red River Jig step is universal, dancers always incorporate their own fancy steps (there are about 50 dance steps used in the jig, and the fancy steps often help reveal the dancer's home community).

As the dancers tire, new dancers jump in and take their place, keeping the dancing alive for hours.